GOODBYE PAPPA

GOODBYE
PAPPA

Una Leavy

Illustrated by
Jennifer Eachus

ORCHARD BOOKS

for Paula
U.L.

for Joel and Jack
J.E.

Orchard Books
96 Leonard Street, London EC2A 4XD
Orchard Books Australia
14 Mars Road, Lane Cove, NSW 2066
First published in Great Britain in 1996
This edition published in 1999
Text © Una Leavy 1996
Illustrations © Jennifer Eachus 1996
ISBN 1 85213 713 4 (hardback)
ISBN 1 84121 083 8 (paperback)
The right of Una Leavy to be identified as the author and Jennifer Eachus
to be identified as the illustrator has been asserted by them in accordance with
the Copyright, Designs and Patents Act, 1988.
A CIP catalogue record for this book is available from the British Library.
1 3 5 7 9 10 8 6 4 2 (hardback)
3 5 7 9 10 8 6 4 2 (paperback)
Printed in Belgium

In Pappa's house the boys wake early.
Sun sneaks in the window.
Soft wind makes the curtains billow.
A bucket rattles.
"Who's coming to look for mushrooms?" Pappa asks.

Over the fields they go – Shane and Peter and Pappa.
Cocks crow, wisps of smoke curl up.
The boys run to keep up with Pappa's step.
The mushrooms grow in cool dark nooks.
They pick them as quickly as they can.
"Mushrooms for breakfast," Pappa says.
Nanna fries them on the pan.

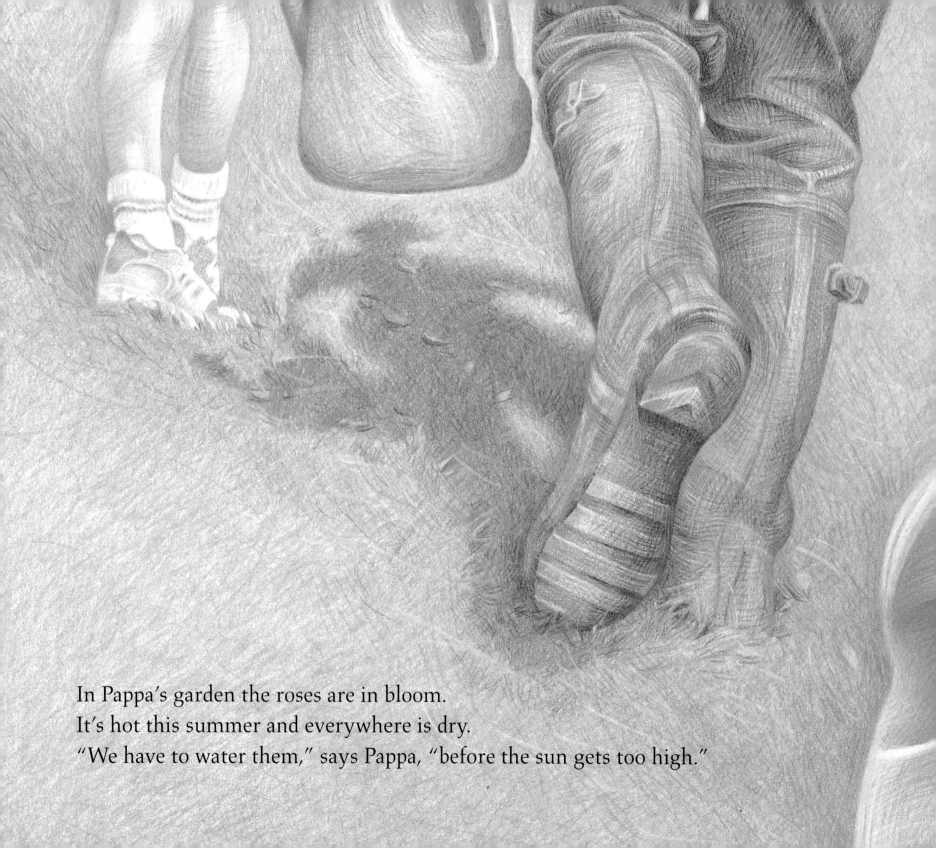

In Pappa's garden the roses are in bloom.
It's hot this summer and everywhere is dry.
"We have to water them," says Pappa, "before the sun gets too high."

Now Pappa makes a path.
He lays the slabs of red and grey beside the cabbage rows.
"I need cement," he says. "Let's go to town."
The boys hop in the car.
It isn't far and Pappa waves to everyone.

Shane and Peter wander round the shop.

There's lots to see – cement and tools and nails.

Then Pappa says, "Who'd like some ice-cream?"

Near Pappa's house a lazy river flows.
Shane and Peter want to go to look for water-hens.
There's none today but Pappa holds them tightly
to see swans gliding between the reeds.
In Pappa's garden there's a hen-run.
Six brown hens grumble and complain.
Shane and Peter bring the eggs in.

It's getting late, the stars are out.
It's almost time for bed.
Pappa takes down the accordion.
Shane and Peter sit in their pyjamas.
They drink their milk and listen while he plays.
He knows their favourite tunes and many more.
His hands fly in and out, his foot thumps on the floor.

Outside the moon hangs round and yellow.
Lying in bed, scraps of music linger in their heads.
Goodnight, Pappa.

On Friday, Shane and Peter have to go home.
Mum takes some photos.
The last thing they see is Pappa's red tee-shirt by the gate.
Goodbye, Pappa . . .

Some days later the phone rang.
It's Uncle Jim.
"Pappa died this morning."

Next week they thank God for Pappa's life.
Dad and his brothers carry Pappa on their shoulders.
Shane and Peter put flowers on the grave.
Dad's crying.

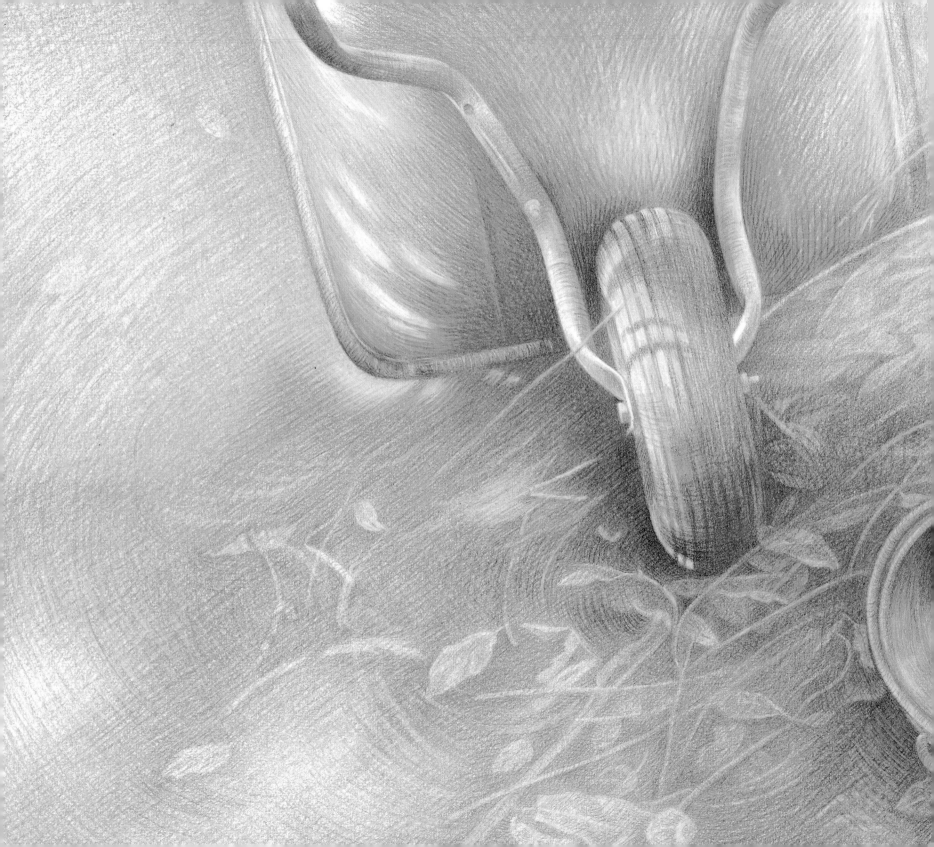

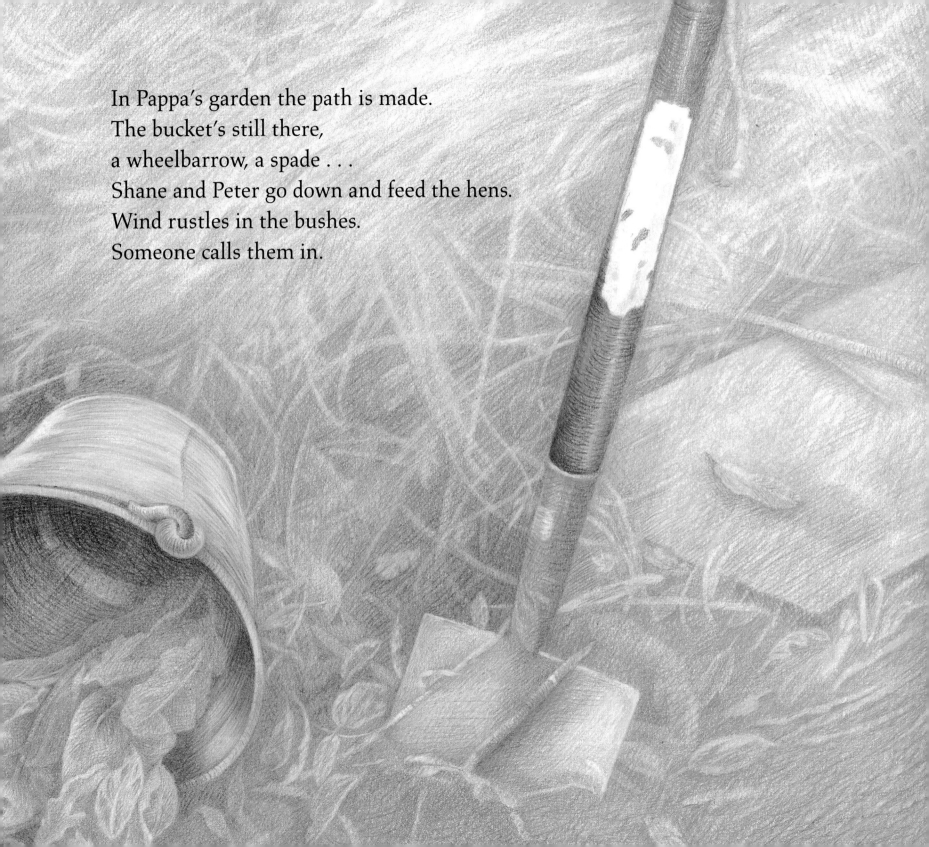

In Pappa's garden the path is made.
The bucket's still there,
a wheelbarrow, a spade . . .
Shane and Peter go down and feed the hens.
Wind rustles in the bushes.
Someone calls them in.

It's getting late, the stars are out.
It's almost time for bed.
They sit in their pyjamas and drink milk.

In Pappa's house Shane and Peter go to bed,
but Peter is afraid.
Mum says, "Don't be scared, Pappa loved you.
Think of all the happy times you had."

Outside the moon hangs round and yellow.
Soft wind makes the curtains billow.
Scraps of music linger in their heads . . .

Goodbye, Pappa . . .